I0538331

Make Fairyland Great Again

FRACTURED FABLES FOR A NATIONAL NIGHTMARE

N.T.O. ZAMBONI

MAKE FAIRYLAND GREAT AGAIN is a work of fiction, believe me.

All tales and morals, incidents and accidents, and all characters—with the exception of a few well-known public monsters—are huge, beautiful products of the storytelling tradition, the collective unconscious, and the author's super-classy imagination and are not to be construed as real. Where real-life public figures appear, the allegories, incidents, and dialogues concerning those persons are so, so fictional and are not intended to depict actual events or to change the tremendously fantastical nature of this work.

In all other respects, any resemblance to persons living or dead is either awkwardly coincidental or entirely satirical, big league.

Copyright © 2016 by NTO Zamboni

All rights reserved.

Published by Grab Them By The Press
Zamboni, NTO.
Make Fairyland Great Again:
Fractured Fables for a National Nightmare

1 Fairytales, Folktales, Legends and Mythology
2 Fiction/Satire
3 Philosophy/Good & Evil

ISBN-13: 978-0692820506
ISBN-10: 0692820507

Other Tremendous Numbers:
99847-520981-34
$915,729,293
KJ 197-324h

"We're going to have to do certain things that were frankly unthinkable a year ago."

The Ant and the Grasshopper

One fine summer afternoon, Grasshopper danced along a sunny path, past raspberry bushes heavy with fruit. He sang and chirped, and gobbled the warm, sweet berries. Then he laughed, watching a row of ants trudge past, carrying kernels of corn toward their colony.

"You are good, hard workers!" Grasshopper said. "Look at you, doing jobs that grasshoppers won't!"

"We have to fill our larder for the winter," one Ant told him. "So when the snow covers the ground we'll still have food to eat."

"The winter's a long way off!" Grasshopper popped another raspberry into his mouth. "There's no reason to worry. I've got plenty."

"We must plan ahead, just in case."

"That's fine for you," Grasshopper chuckled. "But the beauty of me is that I'm rich in berries."

"You should save for the winter, too," the Ant scolded. "For yourself and all the other grasshoppers."

"Why bother?" chirped the Grasshopper. "You've got more than enough."

"You're not going to contribute?" the Ant asked, slightly shocked.

"That makes me smart," Grasshopper announced, and hopped merrily away.

Over the next few weeks, the raspberry bushes gave fewer and fewer berries, until they finally gave none at all. Flurries of snow covered the field, and Grasshopper went knocking on the door of the ant colony.

"Give me some corn," he said.

The Ant tsked. "You should have saved your—"

"I'll protect your jobs!" Grasshopper shouted into the ant colony. "You're losing! Your Ant Queen is so stupid. Everyone in the field is laughing at you. You're living hand-to-mandible, struggling just to get by. You're losing. So, so stupid! Working all summer just to stock your larder."

"We need to stock the larder!" the Ant said. "Now that winter is here—"

"The whole concept of winter," Grasshopper scoffed, "was created by Aardvark. What the hell do you have to lose? Give me your corn, and I'll pay you in berries."

So a group of ants led Grasshopper to the larder, where he stuffed himself until his abdomen bulged and only a few kernels remained.

"Now where are our berries?" the ants asked.

"I'm not paying you."

"But you promised—"

"Wrong!" Grasshopper told them. "You did a job that's not good. Very not good. I don't pay for shoddy work. That's what your whole colony should do."

"All of our corn is gone!" the ants wailed.

N.T.O. Zamboni

"Didn't I say that your Ant Queen is stupid? After all your hard work, you're still losing. Losing all the time."

"We're going to starve," the ants moaned. "Oh, think of the poor pupae."

"You want food? The honeybees are taking your food. They're taking your corn. I love the honeybees, but they're killing you."

"The—the honeybees?" the ants said. "They're just like us, hard workers who raise large broods. Except, instead of saving corn in a larder for winter, they save honey in a comb."

"'Corn, winter, larder,'" Grasshopper scoffed. "You've got to get rid of all these rules. These rules are destroying you. You can't breathe. You cannot breathe."

"We can't eat," the first Ant grumbled. "Because you hogged all our food."

"You want to eat? Put me in charge, and you are going to start eating again. You'll have so much eating you'll get bored of food. Look at me, how my abdomen bulges. I'll get you so much food. So, so much."

Now, the ants prided them on one thing above all else: they were a shining city upon an anthill, where every ant was created equal.

So they held a vote.

The ants who supported Grasshopper marched into a warm and spacious chamber nearby. The ants who supported the Ant Queen marched into a cold and cramped one across the colony.

When the votes were counted, sixty-two ants supported Grasshopper.

Only sixty-five ants supported the Queen, though, so Grasshopper won!

"Wait a second," the first Ant said. "Isn't sixty-five more than sixty-two?"

"Not how we do math," said the other ants.

"Isn't that a problem?" the first Ant asked. "For a shining city on an anthill?"

"It's a huge problem," said the ants whose votes counted more than anyone else's. "We're sick of feeling powerless."

The Emperor's New Clothes

In a fine city on a craggy coast, lofty towers rose overhead and grassy parks spread wide between the avenues. At all hours of day and night, the city rang with music and trade, art and sport. And in the commercial district, bustling boulevards echoed with the cries of fishmongers, costermongers, and ironmongers.

Except one peddler didn't shout in the boulevards.

One peddler wasn't allowed.

He woke early every morning to secure a good spot for his stall, and every morning the other vendors chased him into an alley, between a heap of refuse and a tannery wall.

"Unfair!" he muttered. "I'm the real victim here ..."

He glowered at the other peddlers. Selling fish, apples, and iron was easy! But he was a hatemonger, and peddling hate took real effort. Even people who enjoyed a good, bracing hate in private still shied away from buying his wares in bulk—or in public.

The hatemonger scraped together a meager living from a small-but-fervent following, until one day his best customer pulled him aside. This customer was a clever man named Bartholomew, and he suggested a plan.

"The Emperor," Bright Bart said, "is a shallow, vain man. He loves nothing except himself, and is loved by nobody except himself."

"How can a man like that help our cause?" the hatemonger asked. "We are men of principle and purpose, not self-regard."

"We'll use his vanity to make him our puppet."

So they bought two looms and began to weave a web. Not of cloth, but of lies. They spread word that they were super-classy weavers, the most popular and high-energy weavers in the city. Soon the palace buzzed with the news, and the Emperor summoned the 'weavers' to meet him in the throne room.

"We weave the most amazing clothes, Your Magnificence," Bright Bart told him. "The colors will make your head spin, believe me. And the patterns? Huge. Huge patterns. Beautiful. "

"Tremendous," the hatemonger said, then lowered his voice. "And that's not all, Your Worship."

"What?" the Emperor asked, absently stroking his daughter, who was sitting on his knee. "What else is there?"

"We only use the rarest fabric, Your Supremacy," Bright Bart said. "Fabric so very, very great that it's invisible to anyone who isn't great."

The courtiers gasped in amazement, but the Emperor merely said, "I've heard of that fabric. I know all about it. I have so much knowledge, I know more than anyone."

"Of course, Your Perfection." Bright Bart bowed, and then addressed the courtiers. "You lesser lights may not understand exactly how useful this material is. Our fabric is utterly solid and impeccably sourced ... yet absolutely invisible to anyone who is disgusting or low-energy."

N.T.O. Zamboni

"It cannot be seen by losers or clowns," the hatemonger added, "nor by anyone who is third-rate."

"What we weave on our loom is the truth," Bright Bart told the courtiers. "For those of superior blood and unfettered sight, we embroider everything except the facts."

"You will see the world as it truly is," the hatemonger promised. "For we never cut our cloth on the bias."

The Emperor rubbed his stubby hands together. Using this wondrous fabric, he could easily check if any of his people were losers or dum-dums.

"Make me your finest outfit!" he declared, and told his treasurer to give the weavers a chest overflowing with gold.

"Yes, Your Magnificence," the treasurer said, though knowing his Emperor well, he only gave the weavers a promissory note.

The so-called weavers didn't care: men of principle don't work for a payment, but for a cause. They were hatemongers, and hate does not mong itself. So they set up the two looms and pretended to weave, though they used no thread save that of their curdled imaginations. They danced around the empty looms, making minute adjustments and sweeping generalizations.

For weeks they wefted and wove. Word of their unstinting drudgery spread through the palace to the city, until every one of the Emperor's subjects knew about the wonderful properties of their cloth.

After a time, the Emperor wondered how his new garments were coming along. Did he feel a faint sense of unease, that perhaps he wouldn't see the new clothes? A niggling worry that he would prove to be a loser or a clown?

No.

Not even for the tiniest fraction of an underfed second.

Still, he was curious. Not just for himself, but because he enjoyed a spectacle—and he knew that his subjects were impatient to discover which of their so-called friends were disgusting pigs and low-energy losers.

"I'll send my old guard to have a look," the Emperor decided. "I can trust him, for he grovels better than anyone in the palace, even the Scribe."

"You called, Your Highness?" the Scribe simpered, stepping forward.

The Emperor scowled at the smug, ink-stained wretch. "Go with my old guard to inspect the weavers' work. I can't stand the sight of your ugly face."

So the old guard knocked on the workroom door while the Scribe stood beside him, quill hovering over parchment.

"Before you come in," called the hatemonger, "promise us one thing."

"What's that?" the old guard asked.

"Don't be too kind," the hatemonger told him through the door. "If you spot a single flaw, you must tell us immediately."

"Of course," the old guard said, relieved at this trivial request. After all, he prided himself on his hard-won ability to never spot a serious flaw in any respectable party.

Bright Bart ushered him and the Scribe inside. "The pattern is amazing," Bart said. "The very, very best. And the colors are beautiful, believe me. So beautiful."

The old guard stared at the empty looms, a brittle smile covering the breaking of his heart. He'd always suspected the truth, but he'd never known before: he truly was a loser, a third-rate clown. Without the Emperor, he was worth nothing at all.

Still, before he said anything, he glanced nervously at the Scribe. Maybe—he barely dared hope—maybe the looms truly were empty?

N.T.O. Zamboni

"What do you think?" the Scribe asked him.

"Oh!" The old guard swallowed. "Um. It's tremendous? So, so amazing?"

"How very true!" the hatemonger said.

The old guard took comfort from the scratching of the Scribe's quill, as the ink-stained functionary recorded his words. After all, if the Scribe saw empty looms, he wouldn't simply transcribe the quote, would he?

Of course not. The very idea was laughable.

Bright Bart told the old guard about the 'clothes' in lurid detail, mentioning every imaginary seam and non-existent button. The old guard memorized his words, while the Scribe recorded every boast and brag. And when they returned to the throne room and repeated the breathless description to the Emperor, the courtiers fluttered with excitement.

The Emperor decided he'd wait no longer. With his court at his heels, he rushed to the workroom to see for himself.

"So beautiful!" the old guard cried, throwing the doors wide. "Amazing! Terrific!"

For a terrible moment, the courtiers stared in dismay— then they broke into a chorus of praise, each one seeking to prove that they, at least, were high energy and first rate.

The Emperor approached the empty looms, his brow furrowed. The courtiers quieted. Even the hatemonger held his breath as the Emperor circled the workroom.

"At long last," the Emperor thought, "a set of clothes that truly reflects the inner me. An outfit that encapsulates my very soul." For the Emperor could see clothes on the looms, where no thread existed. His self-regard was so mighty that it painted a breathtaking picture for him, shimmering with his favorite colors: red, white, and blue … but mostly white.

"Huge," he uttered, and the room erupted in cheers.

Make Fairyland Great Again

"Your Superlativeness," said his old guard. "Perhaps you'll grace the city by wearing your new clothes during the procession tomorrow?"

The Emperor agreed, and the 'weavers' worked through the night, inventing a few last challenges for themselves, then proposing a few final solutions. And as dawn broke, they finally announced, "The Emperor's new clothes are ready!"

When the Emperor entered, the 'weavers' bowed low and gestured to the empty racks. "Here are the trousers, Your Magnificence," Bright Bart said. "Here is the shirt and the belt, here the hood and here the robe."

"All of them together as light as a spider web," the hatemonger added.

"Look how it sways," one courtier gasped. "So delicate, so airy."

"And the colors!" another gushed. "Like an autumn sunset over a lavender field."

"Like the fresh fall of snow," Bright Bart murmured, "over a wintry field."

With a steady stream of flattery, the 'weavers' pretended to dress the Emperor. When they finally stepped away, the Emperor surveyed his naked self in the long mirror … and gasped in delight. And after a scant hour enjoying his court's groveling praise, the Emperor marched from the palace, leading the procession through the streets.

Nobody in the city wished to be proven a loser or clown, of course. So the gathered throngs cried, "The Emperor's new clothes are beautiful! They fit him so great! The best!"

"Look at his long train!" called the people leaning from the windows. "That's the longest train. Nobody's ever had a longer train!"

Praise and exultation sounded all around ... except from the costermonger. "He's naked!" she blurted. "He's not wearing anything!"

The courtiers sneered and the guardsmen snorted, but whispers spread like wildfire: "Someone says the Emperor is naked! He's not wearing anything at all!"

"There isn't a single stitch on his flabby bum!" the iron-monger agreed.

"And small hands or no," the fishmonger tittered, "apparently there is a problem. I guarantee it."

Neighbors turned to neighbors. Friends turned to friends. Was it true? Were they not lightweight losers and disgusting pigs? Could they trust what they saw with their own eyes? In a moment, half of the crowd started shouting, "The Emperor has no clothes! The Emperor has no clothes!"

Laughter rippled through the streets ... until the rest of the crowd jeered, "Liars! Crooked liars! He is wearing clothes! The best clothes!"

"You losers just can't see his clothes," the hatemonger called, pushing forward. "Because you're terrible, disgusting people."

"Look at him!" the fishmonger said. "He's naked."

"Treason!" cried Bright Bart. "Who dares mock the Emperor?"

"Ask anyone!" the ironmonger shouted. "Ask ... ask the Scribe!"

The crowd turned to the Scribe, who puffed out his chest and stroked his chin. He looked to the costermonger, then to the hatemonger. He consulted his parchment for a thoughtful moment then gazed at the Emperor, standing naked in front of the parade.

"Tell us!" the costermonger demanded. "Is the Emperor wearing clothes?"

Make Fairyland Great Again

"Some claim he is," the Scribe informed her. "And some claim he's not."

"I'd like to punch them in the face!" the Emperor bellowed, his jowls wobbling. "So obnoxious! So loud! Treat them very, very rough. They ought to be carried out on stretchers!"

"Your wish is our command!" the hatemonger cried, and he and Bright Bart beat the costermonger with cudgels until her bones snapped.

"I hate to intrude, Emperor," the Scribe said, with a trace of alarm. "But perhaps you should stop them?"

"My followers have tremendous love for their country," the Emperor explained. "They're very passionate, and they're sick of losing."

While the costermonger bled to death, Bright Bart took the old guard's place at the Emperor's side. He bowed his head in perfect deference, whispering assurances of loyalty into his puppet's ear. Meanwhile, the hatemonger glared at the frightened crowd. Why weren't they cheering louder? Why did they still resent him, after everything he'd done?

"I'm the real victim here," he muttered.

And the Emperor led the procession away, his new clothes resplendent in the sunshine.

Ali Baba and the Forty Thieves

Once upon a time, a cheerful fat man married a cheerful fat woman, while his sour skinny brother took a sour skinny wife.

The fat brother was named Ali Baba, and he and his wife spent their money as soon as they earned it. They invited dozens of guests to lavish, all-night feasts, they hosted costume balls and poetry readings, they attended dockside concerts and supported religious festivals.

"He wastes all his money," his brother, Kasim, gloated to his wife, in their cold, bare house. "While we hoard all of ours."

"Your brother is foolish," his wife said, skinnily. "And deserves whatever happens to him."

"I hope he doesn't expect me to help," Kasim said, though he dreamed every night of Ali Baba begging for a handout, just so he'd have the opportunity to refuse.

But Ali Baba didn't expect help. Every day he'd cheerfully take his three donkeys into the forest to collect brush to sell at the market. And every evening, he and his wife would cheerfully spend what he earned on guest and neighbors, on sweets and song.

Then one day, as Ali Baby was wandering the forest looking for dropwood, he heard the clipclop of hooves.

"Bandits!" he gasped, and pulled his donkeys into the underbrush.

The horses trotted closer and

> ## DISCONTINUED IN ACCORDANCE WITH THE
> ## 'EXTREME VETTING' GUIDELINES OF
> ## THE DEPARTMENT OF JUSTICE

N.T.O. Zamboni

The Frog Prince

In the old days, when dreams still came true, there lived a princess who loved life, liberty, and the pursuit of her favorite toy, a gleaming golden ball.

In rainy weather, she rolled her golden ball along the grand hallways of the palace and raced it down the wide, winding stairways. On sunny days, she ran outside to throw the ball ever higher, her skirts swishing as she rushed to catch it before it landed. She treasured her ball more than her gowns or crowns—even more than her towns, which sometimes alarmed her with loud noises and boisterous crowds.

Her golden ball never grew heated or rough. It remained always smooth and cool, and formed the most perfect union with her palm.

As it happens, an ancient lime-tree loomed on the fringes of the manicured palace lawns, and an old well waited in the shade of its branches to refresh passers-by. One fateful afternoon, the princess threw her golden ball higher than ever, and instead of falling gently into her hand it vanished into the mouth of the well and was lost to sight.

The young princess wept bitterly, until a voice croaked, "Why are you crying, King's daughter?"

"I—I dropped my golden ball into the well."

"Well, well, well," the voice said.

When the princess wiped the tears from her eyes, she saw a frog stretching his warty, wide-mouthed, bulge-eyed head from the water. "Y-you're a frog!" she blurted.

"What I am is a prince," the frog told her. "The richest prince anywhere. So, so rich. My treasure rooms would make your head spin like a top."

"I don't want a top!" the princess wailed. "I want my golden ball!"

"You want to feel great again?" the frog suggested.

"I do! Won't you help me? And in return, I'll help you! After all, you ... you want to feel human again, don't you?"

"Let us make a deal," the frog said, not quite agreeing.

The princess leaned forward. "Yes?"

"I'll fetch your golden ball if you'll bring me to the palace—"

"Done!"

"—and help me," the frog continued, "until there's no hint of difference between myself and a human courtier."

"Happily!" the princess cried. "Soon you shall act as fine as the finest noble."

The frog sank beneath the surface of the water. A few moments passed, and then the golden ball burst from the well and landed at the princess's slippered feet. Laughing with delight, she scooped up the ball into one hand and the frog into the other, and—

"Oh!" she cried, with a shiver. "You're terribly slimy!"

"I'm the slimiest," the frog replied. "Everyone agrees."

"And quite lumpy."

"With the best lumps," the frog boasted. "And the most."

N.T.O. Zamboni

"You're clammy too, and your skin is a ghastly green."

"Very, very cl—" the frog started, before flicking his tongue at a passing fly.

When he munched on his plump, wriggling snack, the princess almost threw him back into the well. But she'd been raised to be a polite princess, and a promise is a promise, so off she went to the palace with the frog tucked wetly under her arm. She played with him beside her, chasing her golden ball. She slept with him beside her, snoring on a tiny pillow. And she taught him the arts of charity and compassion, of politeness and honesty, of loyalty and modesty.

Yet he didn't improve.

"This is rigged!" he croaked at her. "You let the courtiers insult me."

"I don't! I didn't even scold you for wetting the bed!"

"Unfair!" he ribbeted. "Dishonest, sleazy."

"And that time you slimed the floor—"

"Me? The courtiers are slime! They're sick, and they're making your kingdom sick. Was your vow to me an outright lie? Do you deny the fact that you promised to help me?"

"Of course not! If I pride myself on one thing, it is that I always choose a fact over a truth."

"Then you must let me croak for myself!" the frog said. "Bring me to the Great Hall every night. Defer to me when I speak, then repeat my words in your dulcet voice, that I might mingle better with the courtiers until there is no difference between us."

"The Great Hall?" The princess fiddled with her golden ball. "During mealtimes?"

"Did you not vow to treat me precisely as you'd treat a human prince?"

She didn't remember promising that exactly, but over the next few weeks she did as he asked. She escorted the frog into the Great Hall every night for dinner. She hushed anyone who interrupted him, and she repeated his low croaking in her lovely, musical tones. And sure enough, she soon noticed a difference around the palace.

Where once the frog seemed repugnantly warty, he now seemed pleasantly textured.

Where once he seemed unnaturally hued, he now seemed pleasingly colored.

Where once he seemed revolting in his habits, he now seemed prettily-behaved.

So the frog's wish came true. The princess could detect no difference between him and any of the courtiers. For now, everyone in the palace was lumpy, slimy, and green. The corridors of power swarmed with wide-mouthed, bulge-eyed faces.

As for the princess, she felt a glow of satisfaction that she'd kept her vow. She tossed her golden ball into the air, then caught it with a flick of her sticky tongue.

N.T.O. Zamboni

Rumplestiltskin

Once there was a miller in a bustling castle town who thought he was better than ordinary peasants, as millers so often did. After all, he owned a flourishing business on the edge of town, while they labored in the fields. Still, he worked hard, doffed his cap in church, and often helped the needy and the sick.

Until one year, when the King built a newfangled watermill across town, which ground grain thrice as fast as his mill, and twice as cheap.

The peasants rejoined, but the miller's custom dwindled. A few farmers still brought grain to him, and he still lived better than any rude peasant ... but it rankled.

He'd long dreamed of passing a thriving business to his son. He'd accepted that he'd never have a son—his wife died after blessing him with only a daughter—but now he couldn't pass along anything better than a declining business, getting a bit worse every year.

And why? Because the King meddled in his affairs, and the peasants lacked loyalty.

From time to time, the miller met the King, and naturally the conversation turned to milling. The King, wrapped in fine linen and smelling of spiced oranges instead of honest labor, bragged about the watermill; how fast and cheap, and how wonderful for the peasants!

"That's nothing," the miller said, bitterly. "My daughter can spin straw into gold."

"No!" the King gasped. "Imagine all the good I can do with storerooms full of gold! Send her to me at once."

And so the miller did.

When the girl arrived in the palace, the King gave her a spinning wheel and two reels, then gestured to bales of straw. "And now, young miss, if you please, set to work!"

"I beg your pardon, Your Majesty," the girl said, with a pretty curtsy. "I'll need some cotton, flax, or jute."

"What is this?" the King asked. "I thought all you needed was straw!"

The girl smiled gently. "Oh, no, Your Majesty. That's just my father's way of speaking. I'm sorry for the misunderstanding. Still, I'm counted an excellent spinner, and I vow to do my best."

And so the King (disgruntled but wiser for the lesson in maintaining realistic expectations) sent for flax, and let the miller's daughter spin. Well, she'd spoken the truth: she was a superb spinner. Strong, smooth yarn unfurled from her wheel at such a rate that she alone could supply two weavers.

Soon the King was making a modest profit from her services, which pleased him greatly. In fact, he fell a little in love with the miller's daughter, and enjoyed whiling away the odd hour chatting with her while she spun.

She fell a little in love with him, too. The King was sheltered, it's true, slightly silly, and a bit naive. Still, he cared deeply for his kingdom and always strove to improve the lives of his subjects—even if his 'sweeping' plans usually erred on the side of timidity.

The miller's daughter labored ever harder for her beloved King, until one night while working at the wheel she heard a strange bingbing-bongbong-bingbingbing!

Looking about, she startled at the sight of a tiny man with beefy hands standing beside her. "Oh!"

"Good evening, Mistress Miller!" said the tiny man. "Why are you working so late?"

"I wish to please the King," she told him. "To help him improve his kingdom."

"And you think this is the best way?" the tiny man asked, his scrollwork hair glinting in the lamplight. "By spinning cotton into yarn?"

"Why, yes, I do!" she said.

"If you want to make this kingdom great," the tiny man told her, "you should spin straw into gold."

"I should," agreed the girl, "but nobody can perform such a miraculous feat."

"I happen to be the best spinner in the world," the tiny man said, waving his beefy hands. "I've won so many awards And I shall spin this straw—" he gestured to a forgotten bale. "—into gold!"

"That's wonderful," the girl told him, humoring the poor fellow a little.

"Then the King will make the kingdom great again."

"Yes, um ..." the girl hesitated. "Like it says on your hat."

So the tiny man grabbed a beefy handful of straw and shoved it into the wheel. Whirr, whirr, whirr, said the wheel, and the reel was full of golden straw. Whirr, whirr, whirr, and the second reel was full, too!

The amazed girl ran for the King and told him the tale. Thrilled beyond measure, he followed her back to the workroom. The tiny man was gone, but every inch of straw was glistening and golden.

The King gasped in awe. "Stupendous."

"Oh, Your Majesty," the girl cried. "I'm so sorry! If you look closer, you'll see that the straw is not truly gold, but merely dipped in golden paint."

"But—but why would the little man do that?"

"I've no notion! He is clearly a charlatan—but such an obvious one! Praise the heavens that he is neither clever nor dangerous."

The King shook with laughter. First he'd been fooled by 'straw into gold,' and now she had! He swept the miller's daughter into his arms, and soon she became his Queen.

A year later she was blessed with a beautiful baby girl, and rarely thought about the odd-looking little buffoon. Until one night in her bedchamber she heard the sound again: bingbing-bongbong-bingbingbing!

The tiny man with beefy hands appeared beside the cradle. "Now give me what you promised," he told the Queen.

"Pardon me?" the Queen said. "I didn't promise you anything for your gold-colored straw."

"Believe me, you promised," he cackled, and grabbed the baby. "You promised me your first-born child!"

"I didn't!" she said, her heart unraveling in her chest. "I never did!"

"I have the world's greatest memory," the tiny man said, starting to vanish with the baby in his arms. "It's one thing everyone agrees on."

"No, please!" the Queen wept, falling to her knees. "I beg of you, leave my daughter!"

"Very well," he said, returning the baby to the cradle. "If you discover my name in three days, you may keep the girl."

So the Queen thought of all the names she'd ever heard, and sent messengers across the land to find new ones. When the tiny man came the next day with a bingbing-bong-bong-bingbingbing, she began with Benito and Hermann, and she listed names until her throat grew hoarse.

To every one, the tiny man said, "Wrong!"

On the second day, the Queen listed all the uncommon and curious names she'd heard. "Perhaps your name is Babyfingers or Bannonboy, Asstrumpet or Pencelicker?"

But the tiny man always answered, "Wrong!"

On the third day, the messenger told the Queen, "I still haven't found a new name, but I did find a tiny, vulgar house, all painted in gold, and heard a tiny man singing—

> *Today I fake, tomorrow I spew,*
> *The next I'll have the young Queen's child.*
> *Ha! Glad am I that no one knew*
> *That Rumpelstiltskin I am styled.*

The Queen thanked the messenger profusely, faint with relief that her daughter was saved.

When Rumplestilkskin returned that night, he said, "Now, Mistress Queen, what is my name?"

She pretended to ponder. "Is it Bobby or Rick or Chris or Marco?"

"Wrong!" Rumplestilskin cried, hopping in glee.

"Is it Lindsey or Scott, Jeb or Rand?"

"Now you're just being cruel," he said.

"Then perhaps your name is Rumpelstiltskin?"

The tiny man stamped his tiny foot. "How did you hear? How do you know?"

"That doesn't matter," the Queen said. "Now leave me alone."

Make Fairyland Great Again

"I will!" Rumplestiltskin waved a beefy hand and the baby appeared in his arms. "But I'm taking your daughter with me!"

"You can't!" the Queen said. "You promised not to take her if I discovered your name."

"I never said that!"

"You did! You said that if I—"

"In ten years, I'll be schlonging her!" Rumplestiltskin giggled. Then he vanished with the bawling infant, who was never seen again.

And that is why a King must never meddle in a miller's business.

The Pied Piper

Once upon a time, a swarm of rats infested a pretty town beside a rushing river. At first, nobody cared. The mill-wheels still turned in the swift currents, the vendors still hawked goods in sunny markets.

But these weren't ordinary rats. These rats fought the dogs and killed the cats; they made nests in the women's hats. They raided the storerooms and spread fear of rabies; they even took bites out of slumbering babies.

The people gathered in the town square, shouting for the mayor. "Kill the rats!" a cobbler called. "Wipe them out!"

"They spread disease!" a farmer yelled. "Get rid of them."

The mayor agreed; everyone agreed. The rats were dangerous. So she told the townsfolk to patrol the streets while the town guard scoured the sewers.

After a bloody season of rat-hunting, the vermin fled to the docks ... and the people gathered in the square again.

"This is even worse!" the cobbler said. "The docks are full of rats—they aren't even hiding anymore!"

"At least they're not making nests in hats and killing cats," the mayor said, "or nibbling on our little sprats."

Her words calmed the people ... for a time. Yet with everyone patrolling the streets, the mill-wheels stopped turning and only a few vendors still hawked goods in the markets. The price of bread rose, while rats scuttled in the shadows.

Then a stranger strolled down the long stairway leading to the heart of town, his face multi-colored and his hair a lacquered pelt. He strew copper coins across the cobbled streets until a crowd assembled to greet him.

"What ails this once-great town?" he asked.

The townsfolk told him their troubles: the rats, the cats, the markets and the docks.

"Your worries are over!" the stranger said, with a smile. "I'll fix everything. I'm the only one who can. Your leaders are stupid. So dumb! Let me tell you, I'm a really smart guy."

"Will you fix the mills and the markets?" a baker asked. "Will you stop our children from crying and our dreams from dying?"

"Easily. So, so easily. All your troubles are over, mark my words. Put your town in my hands and you'll be great again so fast your heads will spin."

"But ... but how?"

"I am a rat-catcher," the man announced, raising a golden flute in his short-fingered hands. "I am called the Pied Piper, and I will play a tune on my twitter that leads all the rats away. None will remain, in a single day."

"What about the rest of our problems?" a bard asked.

"What caused all this? What was the start of all your problems? The rats!"

"I'm handling the rats," the mayor said, pushing to the front of the crowd.

"Not like I will. I'll kill them all. I'll kill all the dogs and cats, too—"

"What? Why?"

"The dogs and cats know what's going on. Believe me. They know. I'll knock the crap out of them."

"Are you going to drown them?" a little boy asked.

The Pied Piper patted the boy's head. "I'll do more than that. I'll charm them into the countryside and stuff them into sacks full of broken glass."

"The—dogs and cats, too?" the mayor asked. "You can't—"

"Torture works," the Piper said. "Believe me, it works. I'll kill them all. The rats and their families." He sounded a note on his twitter until every eye fell upon his mottled face. "Now, who wants to hire me?"

A hundred voices shouted, "Hire him, hire him!"

"Who doesn't want to hire him?" the mayor asked.

More than a hundred voices shouted, "Don't hire him! He's dangerous!"

And so it was unanimous; the town hired the Pied Piper.

> Into the docks the Piper stepped,
> Smiling first a little smile,
> As if he knew what magic slept,
> In twitter all the while.
> And then like a media adept,
> Vile things the blowhard uttered.
> Until there came a mighty rumbling;
> And from the docks the rats came tumbling.
> Huge rats, small rats, nice rats, mean rats,
> Fat rats, thin rats, dirty rats, clean rats,
> Grave old dogs, young feline friskers,
> Cocking tails and pricking whiskers,
> Brothers, sisters, husbands, wives—
> Followed the Piper for their lives.

Make Fairyland Great Again

The Pied Piper drowned them in the river. The village rejoiced, and when the Piper demanded payment, the mayor obligingly handed over her robe of office.

The Piper settled into his new role, and every time he stepped from town hall the people cheered. Many of them, at least. A few lightweights still grumbled. A few losers still groused: "The mills still don't work, and bread costs more than ever."

"Knock the crap out of them, would you?" the Piper told the crowd. "In the good old days, we treated complaining very, very rough. We've become very weak. The problem is, nobody wants to hurt each other anymore."

"What are you talking about?" the bard asked, aghast. "You're the mayor! You promised you'd fix everything!"

"I'm not looking for bad in your town. I'm a very rational person. I'm a very sane person. I'm not looking for bad. But the level of hatred is so incredible, I actually wonder, why am I doing this? Why am I here?"

"You're here," the bard said, "because you promised you'd stop the children crying!"

The Piper's eyes glinted like copper coins. "Mark my words," he said. "I always keep my promises."

When he twittered his flute, all the town's boys and girls gathered around. He danced them through the gates and into the countryside, where the notes of his song mixed with the tinkling of broken glass.

Sleeping Beauty

In a land beside a shining sea, two Queens—after long years of trying—were blessed with a healthy baby daughter. Overjoyed, they planned a lavish christening for the infant Princess. They bickered about the seating chart (one cousin was too fond of mead, while another was too fond of his opinions), but overall the preparations went smoothly and the invitations were soon sent.

Among the guests were seven good fairies. "Or at least," said one of the queens, "let us call them 'adequate fairies'. Nobody's perfect, but they do try their best."

"Unlike that other fairy," her wife said, meaningfully.

They nodded together over their cooing baby, for the other fairy was spiteful and mean, selfish and greedy and cruel. In fact, she even called herself 'the evil fairy,' just to make people fear her.

Finally, the day of celebration came. The musicians played, the fountains bubbled, and each of the fairies gave a gift to the infant Princess.

The generous, vain fairy gave the gift of beauty.

The clever, critical fairy gave the gift of intelligence.

The brash, sporty fairy gave the gift of athleticism.

The capable, prim fairy gave the gift of discipline.

The fifth fairy gave a copper statue of a robed lady bearing a torch and a tablet.

The smug, accomplished fairy gave the gift of ambition.

And the seventh fairy—

"Stop!" cackled the evil fairy, hunched over the infant Princess. "You didn't invite me, but I'll give a gift just the same."

"Of course you were invited!" the Queens cried, lying desperately. "The royal mail must've lost your—"

"My evil gift is this," the evil fairy said, as dark clouds gathered outside the palace windows. "One day the Princess will prick her finger on a spindle and die."

The Queens sobbed and guests wept, "What has the evil fairy done?"

Except for the cousin with a fondness for his own opinions, who muttered, "Stop referring to her as 'evil'!"

"But I am evil!" the evil fairy cried, and she vanished into the storm front.

"See?" the cousin who enjoyed mead said. "She even calls herself 'evil.'"

"Watch your tongue!" the opinionated cousin snapped. "You overreact to the slightest things. Besides, a prick of the finger won't kill the Princess."

"He's right," said the seventh, forgotten fairy. "For here is my gift: the Princess shall not die if ever she pricks her finger."

"Told you so," the opinionated cousin muttered. "You're all so hysterical."

"She will merely fall into a deep, nightmarish sleep for four tragic years," the seventh fair continued. "Or for eight unimaginably devastating ones, if a mighty voice doesn't wake her."

Afraid for their beloved daughter, the Queens immediately ordered the destruction of every spindle in the land.

Over the next sixteen years the infant Princess grew tall and strong. However, the economy faltered, on account of complex and multicausal systemic weaknesses, and the people became restive, blaming the land's ills on the prohibition of spindles. (Except for the opinionated cousin, who said: "You get what you deserve, for not politely inviting evil into your house.")

At sixteen, the Princess ventured into a palace tower she'd never visited before, and slammed the door behind her. (Although beautiful, smart, athletic, and wise, she was still a teenager, and subject to fits of sullenness.) There she met the evil fairy, in the guise of a Repugnant Prince.

"What is the matter, Your Royal Highness?" asked the Repugnant Prince.

"My mothers treat me like I need a nanny," the Princess grumbled. "And the people are so angry and bitter."

"They're so, so stupid," the Repugnant Prince told her. "Crooked queens are the worst."

The princess found perverse comfort in the prince's words. "My mothers try to make my life better through policies I barely understand," she said to herself, "but the prince is already making my life better by saying what I feel."

"Do you know what the Queens would truly hate?" the Repugnant Prince asked her. "If you pricked your finger on that spindle. That would show them. They'll be sorry they ever neglected you."

"They will!" the princess cried. "They will be sorry!"

So she pricked her finger and fell into a fitful sleep, haunted by horrific dreams.

Make Fairyland Great Again

The people mourned and the sorrowful Queens scoured the land for a 'mighty voice' to wake the princess, searching ceaselessly for a singer, a hymn, and a chorus to break the evil spell.

And the Repugnant Prince? He grabbed the Princess by the pussy as she slept. She didn't stir, but that didn't bother him. He just started kissing her. He didn't even wait. When you're a Prince, you can do anything.

N.T.O. Zamboni

Peter and the Wolf

Young Peter lived in a cottage in a golden forest glade, behind a high fence his father had built to protect him from the wild animals.

One day, when Peter went into the forest, he left the garden gate open. He wandered the sun-dappled paths, whistling a jaunty tune and popping the heads off dandelions, until he came to a pond.

There he spotted a blackbird perched in a berry bush, singing to herself. Peter shivered in disgust. He'd never seen a blackbird before. What was she doing? What was she after?

"Hey, you!" a duck quacked to the blackbird. "You, in the bush! What kind of bird can't swim?"

The blackbird nibbled a berry. "What kind of bird can't swoop and dive, zigzagging through the forest branches?"

"Believe me, I can swoop!" the duck said. "I'm the best at zigging. Nobody zags better than me!"

Peter clapped, pleased with the duck for scolding the strange black bird. He tossed breadcrumbs to reward the brave creature, then sat on the bank and chatted with the duck … until his father rushed into sight.

"What are you doing out here?" his father demanded. "Stop feeding that greedy duck! What if Vlad the Wolf comes out of the forest?"

"I'm not afraid of Vlad!" Peter said.

"You should be," his father told him. "That wolf will try any trick to get into our garden and gobble us up. He's even worse than those lazy blackbirds …"

From that day forth, frightened but fascinated, Peter watched the pond through the slats of the fence.

One afternoon, Peter spotted Vlad prowling from the forest—a wolf so big that he looked more like a bear. At the sight of the huge wolf, the blackbird swooped to a higher branch. But the duck was still angry that Peter's father called him greedy, and paddled closer to the bank.

"Friend wolf," he quacked. "I have a plan. If you and I work togeth—"

Vlad leapt at the duck and swallowed him whole.

Watching from his garden, Peter gasped at the loss of his friend. He fetched a rope, threw open the gate, then raced to the pond and climbed a tree.

Once safe in the branches, he called, "Blackbird, blackbird! Fly into the wolf's mouth to distract him!"

"To tell the truth," the blackbird sang, eying the wolf's sharp teeth, "I'd rather not."

"My father was right!" Peter sniffed. "The blackbirds are lazy and low-energy!"

So he lowered his rope to catch the huge wolf by his tail. However, Vlad merely spun and gave the rope a sharp tug.

N.T.O. Zamboni

Peter fell directly into the wolf's mouth and was swallowed whole. With a toothy grin, Vlad loped through the open gate, ate Peter's father, and made the cottage his new den. And if you listen carefully, you can still hear the duck quacking inside the wolf's belly, blaming everything on the blackbirds.

Hansel and Gretel

A prosperous woodcutter lived with his third wife on the edge of a large forest. The woodcutter enjoyed the finer things in life, and deservedly so. After all, hadn't he expanded his father's property into a thriving business, at roughly the same rate it would've grown if he'd done nothing at all?

Of all the fineries he coveted, the woodcutter prized none more than sweets. Gingerbread, fruit tarts, marzipan and funnel cakes, he loved them equally. So when a band of brigands emptied all the sweet shops of the country, he suffered keenly. However, his suffering lightened somewhat when the Town Watch pounded on his door and gave him someone to blame.

"We tracked the thieves toward the central forest," the chief of the watch informed him. "And the trail leads directly beside your house."

The woodcutter grasped the situation immediately. He was a man of lightning understanding, and never wrong.

"Those children next door are the thieves!" he howled. "Hansel and Gretel."

"Very likely," the chief said. "But the path did continue past—"

The woodcutter raised a hand for silence. "I know by their black souls that they're guilty!"

"Are you certain?" the chief asked.

"I am always certain," the woodcutter told him. "And never in doubt."

"In that case," the chief said, "the punishment is a sentence of—"

"The death penalty!" the woodcutter interrupted. "Nothing less will do!"

"That's not the—"

"What if my customers hear about criminals living so close to my home? They'll shrink from buying my goods. Let me punish these children myself."

He handed over a bag of coins, and the chief agreed.

That night, lying in bed, the woodcutter turned to his wife. "Tomorrow morning, I'll take those black-hearted children into the deepest depths of the forest. I'll leave them there, and they won't be able to find their way home."

"Leave them?" his wife said. "The wild beasts will tear them apart!"

"*They* are the predators," the woodcutter replied.

Outside the window, where they'd been secretly listening, Hansel and Gretel wept bitter tears. "We're doomed!" Gretel said. "We can't refuse to join him, or he'll know what we suspect."

"You'll think of something," Hansel told her. "You always do."

"I haven't a single idea!" Gretel moaned. "Other than dropping white pebbles as we're led into the woods, then following them back home."

"Clever sister!" Hansel said. "That's just what we'll do."

Make Fairyland Great Again

So the next day, as the woodcutter led them into the darkest glades of the forest, they dropped a trail of pebbles. The woodcutter told them to stay near the fire then crept away into the shadows. However, when the moon rose, Hansel and Gretel followed the trail that glittered like newly-minted silver coins all the way back home.

The next day, the woodcutter told them, "We're returning into the woods, children. Try to keep up this time."

"He's going to leave us again," Gretel whispered to Hansel.

"We need more pebbles," Hansel said.

"There aren't any!"

Hansel gulped. "Then ... I guess we'll use breadcrumbs."

"That won't work! Mice will eat them. We need something that shines brightly ..."

"The woodcutter's wife's box of buttons!" Hansel said. "They're shiny."

"And not good for anything except keeping the fabric of society together," Gretel said, which was an old joke that went right over Hansel's head.

Once again, the woodcutter led them into the thickest woodland, then abandoned them to fate. But this time, when Hansel and Gretel looked for their path home, the buttons were gone, stolen by shrieking magpies who didn't care about fabric and couldn't resist shiny objects.

"We're doomed!" Gretel said.

"You'll think of something," Hansel said.

But she didn't.

They walked for days, hiding from beasts and suffering from hunger, until they came upon a house made entirely of sweets. Gingerbread doors stood beneath a flaky roof with licorice gutters. Icing surrounded the windows, and puff pastry bulged in unexpected places.

"Food!" Hansel cried, his mouth watering. "Food!"

"Not just any food," Gretel told him. "This is the stolen pastry!"

"We've found the thieves!"

"And once we find our way home, this will prove our innocence."

Except, of course, the house belonged to a wicked witch, who captured them in a trap designed to appeal to the most infantile appetites. The witch locked Hansel in a cage, and forced Gretel into servitude. For six years.

The day came, though, when Hansel and Gretel escaped. They grabbed gumdrops for provisions and for proof, and fled into the forest. That time, they were not lost. They'd learned a few things over the years, and they followed the constellations into town.

"We're innocent!" they told the chief of the Town Watch.

"We know," he said. "The witch confessed."

"And the woodcutter?" Gretel asked.

The chief brought that worthy man forward and told him, "Remove the hate and rancor from your heart."

"I don't think so!" the woodcutter snarled, snatching the gumdrops from Gretel. "These kids are no angels, believe me. What were they doing in the woods, playing hopscotch?" He gave the chief another bag of coins. "Hang them in the town square."

"Husband, no!" his wife gasped. "Surely if you do that, your customers will shrink from buying your goods!"

"Wrong!" the woodcutter barked, because he'd learned a few things, too. "They'll line up around the block!"

And so he built a beautiful gallows in the center of town. A great, great gallows. The crowd cheered when Hansel and Gretel were hanged to death, and the woodcutter lived happily ever after, raiding the witch's cottage for sweets.

Make Fairyland Great Again

And so he built a beautiful gallows in the center of town. A great, great gallows. The crowd cheered when Hansel and Gretel were hanged to death, and the woodcutter lived happily ever after, raiding the witch's cottage for sweets.

Little Red Riding Hood

A girl named Little Red Riding Hood lived in the city with her father, on a pretty street that echoed with laughter by day and glowed with lamplight by night.

One morning, her father told her, "Take a loaf of bread to Grandma, and see how she's doing. She's been acting oddly lately. Perhaps she's ill."

"Yes, father!" Little Red Riding Hood said, putting the loaf into a basket with a pot of jam.

Her father tsked. "Be careful on the way!"

"Why?" asked Little Red Riding Hood, her eyes widening. "Are there bandits on the road? Are there wolves?"

"No, you silly goose!" Her father chuckled. "Be careful not to spill the jam. Your hood is red, but jam still stains."

So Little Red Riding Hood took off skipping to her grandmother's house. She loved visiting Grandma: she loved Grandma's pies and stories. She loved playing dress-up in Grandma's frocks and hats. She sang happily as she followed the path, stopping to pick hazelnuts and chase butterflies.

When she reached grandmother's house, she knocked. Rat! Tat!

"Who's there?" called her grandmother.

"It's me, Grandma!" she answered. "Little Red Riding Hood! I brought you a loaf of bread that Daddy baked."

"Come in, come in!" Grandma called. "Pull the handle, the latch will give."

"Oh, no!" Little Red Riding Hood thought. "Grandma is so ill that she can't even open the door."

But when she stepped inside, she found her grandmother looking hale and hearty, sitting on her couch watching the antics of a most curious creature: a blonde and leggy animal who paced the rug and purred to grandma.

"What—" Little Red Riding Hood blurted. "I mean who … I mean hello!"

"Sit with me, child, and let me introduce my dearest friend." Grandma patted the couch. "This, my dear, is Fox."

"Pleased to meet you," Little Red Riding Hood said.

Fox smiled with all his teeth. "I am fair and balanced to meet you as well, miss."

Little Red Riding Hood wasn't quite sure what to make of Fox's manner of speaking. Still, she found him fascinating, with his calming voice and his angry eyes.

"I was just telling your grandmother some news about the city," Fox said.

"Oh, good!" Little Red Riding Hood said, pleased to find herself on familiar ground. "I just came from there!"

"My poor child," Grandma murmured.

"They look for trouble in the city," Fox told grandmother. "It's a disgrace, what they get away with. They are full of hate, and crime is at record levels. Some streets are so dangerous that even the City Watch won't enter."

"That's not true!" Little Red Riding Hood said. "None of that is true!"

"Hush, child," her grandmother said. "Fox is speaking."

Little Red Riding Hood quieted, for she'd been raised to treat her elders politely. But as Fox kept speaking, she fancied that she could feel the bite of carnivorous teeth at the end of every sentence, and smell the scent of blood.

"Pardon me," she finally murmured. "I'll just put the bread and jam away ..."

Her grandmother didn't notice when she stepped into the kitchen. Little Red Riding Hood set the kettle to boil, then listened to Fox speaking in the other room.

"There is violence in our streets," he told Grandma. "Disasters are unfolding, the kingdom is in ruins. We don't have much time."

"Oh my goodness," Grandma said, and eagerness mixed in with her sorrow. "Such terrible news!"

"We suffer one humiliation after another," Fox purred, warming to his theme. "There's poverty and corruption at home, war and destruction abroad. Men, women and children are viciously crushed. Families are ripped apart. This is the legacy of the city, and everyone who lives there: death, destruction, terrorism and weakness."

"Grandmother!" Little Red Riding Hood said, bursting from the kitchen. "What big lies you believe!"

"The better to judge you with, my dear."

"Grandmother! What hurtful stereotypes you repeat!"

"The better to fear you with, my dear."

"Grandmother! What a big axe you grind!"

"The better to fix you with, my dear."

"Grandmother! What are you—" Little Red Riding Hood screamed. "No, please! Grandmother!"

Make Fairyland Great Again

Brer Rabbit Earns a Dollar a Minute

Once upon a time, Brer Fox had the best peanut patch. Just terrific. Mark my words. A great, great, great peanut patch. Green vines, ripe peanuts, tremendous.

The other creatures knew that Brer Fox's patch was the best. Their patches were strictly third rate. They had zero peanut cred, and they were jealous. So, so jealous.

All of them except one. Brer Rabbit. The trickster. Crooked Rab, I call him. Lying Rab. Brer Rabbit had mastered the art of the free meal. He waited until the peanuts were ripe, because believe me, he knew something nobody else did: he knew about the hole in the fence around Brer Fox's peanut patch, and every few nights, he'd sneak inside and help himself.

Brer Fox noticed that someone was snatching his peanuts. He poked around, and found the hole in his fence, just the right size for a rabbit. So he set a trap, the best trap. He grabbed a length of rope, then bent a branch of a hickory tree to the ground and weighed it down with a rock.

He made a snare trap with the rope, then went home to wait for morning.

That very night, when crooked Brer Rabbit snuck into the patch to grab some peanuts, he kicked the rock aside. Whoosh! The loop snagged his leg and hauled him into the air. Brer Rabbit was caught!

He dangled upside-down from the hickory branch like a dummy. He kicked and struggled, but couldn't get free. So, so miserable. I love rabbits, nobody loves rabbits more than me, but they're diseased animals, mark my words.

Crooked Brer Rabbit knew that Brer Fox would check the trap in the morning. He struggled, but didn't have enough stamina to escape. And sure enough, along with the first rays of dawn came the sound of lumbering pawsteps in the underbrush.

Brer Rabbit pricked one long ear. "That's Brer Bear!" he said to himself. "If I can convince him that Brer Fox is paying me a dollar a minute to hang here, with a story about—"

"ALL STORIES MATTER!" Brer Crow cawed, swooping into the hickory tree.

"Hush a moment!" Brer Rabbit said. "I'm trying to think—"

"ALL STORIES MATTER!" A murder of crows landed in the branches, giving a raucous: "CAW! CAW-CAW! CAW! ALL STORIES MATTER!"

"Well, I'm in the middle of working on this story," Crooked Brer Rabbit told them, "so if you'd kindly—"

Brer Crow flapped his wings furiously. "ALL STORIES MATTER."

"Fine, yes! But if all stories matter, why don't you let me think on this one? Okay? Okay. I'll tell Brer Bear that I'm working as ... a scarecrow—"

"CAW! ALL STORIES MATTER! CAW! CAW! ALL STORIES MATTER!"

Make Fairyland Great Again

When Brer Rabbit heard Brer Bear lumbering closer, he started feeling a little desperate. "You already said that! Now would you shut your beaks for one minute and let me tell THIS story?"

"WHY ARE YOU SHOUTING? CAW-CAW! SUCH A NASTY RABBIT! ALL STORIES MATTER! ALL STORIES MATTER. NOT YOUR STORIES, ALL STORIES! ALL STORIES MATTER. CAW! CAW-CAW-CAW! ALL STORIES MATTER, ALL STORIES MATTER. ALL STORIES MATTER! CAW!"

And they made such a racket that Brer Fox came running with another length of rope.

The Princess and the Pea

Once upon a time in a land called Gold, there was a Prince who wanted to marry a princess. Not just any princess: he wanted to marry the best princess. A super-luxury princess, the greatest princess in all the world.

So his mother the Queen invited the Princess of Oak to meet her son. Princess Oak played the lute so beautifully that mockingbirds built nests on the grounds of her castle so their hatchlings would hear her music before any other sound.

Princess Oak came into the throne room with her lute and curtseyed to the Prince. "My dear prince," she said, "how delightful to—"

"Look at that face," the Prince snarled to his Advisor. "Would anybody marry that? Can you imagine that, the face our next queen?"

"I beg your pardon—" Princess Oak started.

"Why is she always interrupting?" the Prince barked. "What a dummy!"

"I beg you, my prince," the Advisor murmured. "Do not violate the norms of polite behavior."

"Send her away!" the Prince bellowed.

Next came the Princess of Coral, a young lady with long hair and bright eyes, known for her elegance.

"That is a beautiful piece of ass," the Prince said, with a noble graciousness.

Princess Coral gave a polite smile. "I'm not sure we'd suit, Your Highness, perhaps—"

"Wrong!" the Prince barked. "Rude, obnoxious, and dumb."

"Tsk-tsk," the Advisor murmured.

"Next!" the Prince yelled.

The Princess of Harmony glided into the throne room, and—

"Gold-digger!" the Prince pronounced. "Grotesque. A bimbo."

When Princess Ivy entered—

"Disgusting!" the Prince howled. "A pig!"

"Tut-tut," the Advisor murmured.

Princess Saffron stepped into the throne room and approached the Prince with all the grace of a swan, stunning in a flowing gown. She gave a low and respectful curtsy ... but not low enough.

"Look at that fat, ugly face!" the Prince shouted. "Like a dog. Next!"

"This is Princess Linen," the Queen said. "In her kingdom, she asks herbalists to help the sick. However, some say that she sends royal messages with courier pigeons instead—"

"COURIER PIGEONS?!" the Advisor howled, leaping to his feet. "What manner of horror is this? Pigeon couriers! What sort of monster would use birds in this fashion?"

"Well, I did the same as a princess," the Queen mentioned.

The Advisor wasn't listening. He pounded the floor with his staff until the Prince bellowed, "Such a nasty woman! Lock her up! Lock her up! Next!"

"There are no more," the Queen told her son. "She was the last one."

"Where's daddy?" the Prince asked, sulking on his golden throne. "He'll know what to do."

"Your father is attending a royal klavern," the Queen told him.

"When I'm king I'll hold the klavens here," the Prince said. "And I'll make them my advisors."

"Hm," murmured the Advisor, busy with thoughts of courier pigeons.

That evening, a torrential downpour swept across the land. Lightning flashed, thunder crashed ... and a pounding sounded at the castle door.

Outside stood one last princess. At least, she claimed she was a princess. But what a sight! Water dripped down her face and soaked her hajib, while mud splattered the hem of her gown and her silken slippers.

"Pardon the state of me," she said. "But indeed, I am the Princess of Emerald."

"We shall see about that," the Queen thought.

She commanded her servants to place a single pea on a bedstead and to stack twenty mattresses on top. "Then show this so-called princess into that room, to sleep."

The servants did as they were bidden. Upon entering the bedchamber, Princess Emerald eyed the tall stack of mattresses in surprise. However, being a polite guest, she simply climbed the ladder and settled in for the night.

The next morning, the Queen met the Princess at breakfast. "Good morning, my dear. How did you sleep?"

"Very well, thank you," the Princess replied. After all, what kind of person would complain about sleeping poorly after being generously offered a bed?

"Are you sure?" the Queen asked. "You appear a tiny bit tired."

"I did toss and turn a little," the Princess admitted. "Probably because of the thunder."

"Was it just the thunder that bothered you?" the Queen asked.

"To be perfectly frank," the Princess said, for she'd been raised to be honest as well as polite, "I feel terribly rude saying this, but I hope there's nothing wrong with the bed. It felt as if I were lying on a boulder."

"You are a princess!" The Queen clapped her hands in delight and called Prince Gold into the breakfast room. "This is Princess Emerald. She's everything you want in a wife."

"Almost everything," the Prince said, from around a mouthful of sausages.

The Queen blinked at him. "What's wrong?"

"She's a princess," he said. "And princess are crude, obnoxious pigs."

"Not Princess Emerald! She's not any of those things!"

"Maybe not," the Prince grumbled. "But I'll only consider her if she denounces all princesses for treating me so rudely."

"Of course I condemn rudeness," the Emerald Princess said, firmly. "Rudeness is very wrong."

"And crudeness."

"I condemn crudeness as well."

"And princesses who act like fat, disgusting dogs."

"Er, yes." The princess smiled weakly. "Of course, I can't condone anyone acting like a ... a disgusting dog."

"Then denounce the princesses who acted that way!" the Prince roared.

"I do, I do!" the Princess said. "I denounce everyone who acts in a disgusting manner. You know, Your Majesty, that there is a deplorable minority in every group that behaves poorly, but—"

"Condemn the dummy princesses and the ugly princesses!" Prince Gold spat. "Condemn the nasty ones who think they're better than me."

"I—I condemn them," she said, a little shaken.

"Condemn then louder," the Prince said.

Princess Emerald condemned them louder.

"Now condemn all princesses," he told her. "Every single one of those miserable pigs."

"But I'm a princess!" she said.

"Then I shan't be satisfied," he told her, coldly, "until you condemn yourself."

A Girl and Her Donkey

Once upon a time there was a twelve-year-old girl who lived with her mother and three younger sisters. Her mother worked two jobs to pay for their little house outside of the village. And even though she was still a young woman (for a mother), her hair was gray and her back was stooped.

So one day, the girl said, "Mama, I want to help you."

"Then remember to brush your teeth without being reminded every single night," her mother said.

"I don't mean that!" the girl said. "I want to get a job."

"You're too young."

"Pleeeease," the girl begged. "I'm trying to help, and you always say that everyone should help one other."

The girl pleaded and pleased. Finally, her mother agreed, and prepared a packsack for her, with tortillas and clothes— and of course her toothbrush. The girl loaded the donkey, and her mother wept and prayed as they hugged goodbye.

The girl followed the path toward the city, but she'd never been on her own before. The shadows grew longer and the air colder. When the sun set, she almost lost courage, but then she remembered her mother's tears.

"I will find work!" she vowed to herself.

The next day, leading the donkey through a desolate area, the girl met a woman in a red sash, white shirt, and blue dress.

"Where are you heading, my child?" the woman asked.

"To get a job in the city," the girl answered. "To help my mother."

"Are you brushing your teeth everyday?" the woman asked.

"Yes!" the girl said. "Well, starting tomorrow."

The woman smiled. "Be careful on this road. There are people who will try to steal from you."

"I'm not afraid," the girl said. "Besides, I have nothing for them to steal other than my donkey, and I'll never let him out of my sight."

"Take these three slices of apple pie," the woman told her. "If you meet anyone who wants to join you on your journey, cut one slice in half. Not evenly, though. Make sure one half is bigger than the other."

"I'll do as you say," the girl said, taking the slices of pie. "But ... why?"

"Offer both pieces to the other traveler. If they take the larger one, you'll know that you can't trust them."

The girl laughed and thanked the woman, then tucked the pie into her pack and led her donkey away. That very afternoon, she met a cooper who suggested that they travel together, to make the time pass more easily.

"After all," the cooper said, "nothing else is easy these days."

"What do you mean?" the girl asked, as they fell into step.

"The fancy toffs in the city don't buy many barrels anymore," lamented the cooper. "Instead, they prance around in silken robes, sniffing at ordinary folk like me, cutting our purses and stealing our livelihood."

The girl frowned. "That is poorly done of them!"

"And making my family poorer, too," the cooper said.

After a time, they paused to rest. The girl remembered the woman's words and cut a slice of pie into uneven slices. "Would you like some?" she asked the cooper.

"In the old days, it would be me giving charity," he said, with a merry chuckle, "and a little brown girl like you would've been grateful for my crumbs! How things have changed!"

The girl patted her donkey uncomfortably. "Oh."

"And in the old days, I always had a whole slice of pie to myself," the cooper said, taking the larger piece. "So clearly this one should be mine."

The girl took her leave shortly thereafter, and led her donkey along the winding paths toward the city. Early the next morning, she met a pilgrim woman.

"Shall we travel together?" the woman asked. "There is safety in numbers."

"Yes, thank you," the girl said.

"Where are you going?" the woman asked.

"To the city," the girl told her, "to find work to help my mother."

"Oh, my child!" cried the pilgrim woman. "The city is a den of sin! Nobody goes to the city except godless heathens."

"But I'm not godless," the girl said, "and I'm going to the city."

The woman didn't seem to hear. "They are crude and boorish. Why, there are garish murals of nakedness on every corner!"

The girl blushed. "That's horrible."

"They are horrible, with fleshy lips and groping hands."

"That's even more horrible!" The girl cut her second slice of pie into uneven halves (though sticklers will claim that 'halves' are by definition exactly equal). "Would you like some pie?"

"I deserve the bigger slice," the pilgrim woman thought to herself. "Since I am beset by enemies at every turn, and this child will soon be lost to sin in the city."

She took the larger piece, and the two parted ways.

The next morning, the girl heard a blare of horns and the jingle of bells. She met a jolly man with a brightly-colored cart drawn by horses in golden livery, leading a procession of dancers, including the cooper and the pilgrim.

"Where are you heading, girl?" the jolly man called.

"To look for work in the city," she told him, above the sound of revelry. "To help my mother and my three little—"

"Have you considering modeling?" the jolly man asked.

The girl glanced at the procession, hoping that the pilgrim woman would say something, but yet again she didn't seem to hear.

"I think I'm too young for that," the girl said.

"A good friend of mine throws parties for girls like you," the man called, with a jovial laugh. "And young is how he likes them. The best parties. Believe me."

"Er, would you like some apple pie?" the girl asked, to change the subject, cutting her third slice into unequal halves. "If you're hungry, feel free to—"

"Very nice." The man grabbed the smaller piece. "One for me."

Well, the girl thought, at least he's honest.

The man grabbed the other piece. "And the other for me."

"What are you doing?" she asked,

"I'm winning," he announced, to a fanfare of trumpets.

He pranced in his silken robes to the other side of the cart, which was covered by a garish mural of nakedness. He sniffed at the cooper before cutting his purse, then smacked his fleshy lips and groped the pilgrim.

Make Fairyland Great Again

"What are you doing following this man?" the girl asked the cooper and pilgrim. "He is everything you hate."

"He is everything we love!" they corrected.

"He's crude and boorish, just the sort of fancy toff who sniffs and gropes—"

The jolly man cut her off. "Good luck finding a job, Miss Housekeeping! What a dummy. You'll never get into the city. We built a wall!"

And the man stole the girl's donkey while the cooper and pilgrim kicked out her well-brushed teeth. At least, someone's doing the kicking. I mean, someone's doing it. Who's doing the kicking? Who is doing the kicking?

Jack and the Beanstalk

In a cottage in a rather ordinary village, there lived a rather typical widow. Her husband had died years earlier, in a war that at first she'd supported and then opposed, all without ever changing her opinion.

After years of drought, almost nothing remained in the cottage except the widow's son, Jack, and a good-natured cow who was the best milker in the parish.

Finally, scattered rains fell and crops began to sprout. However, despite these hopeful signs, the widow cried, "Cruel fate! We're out of money, and there's still many months before the harvest! We can't even afford bread. We have to sell the cow or we'll starve."

"Are you sure?" Jack asked. "I mean, if we sell the cow we'll have nothing except the money she fetches, and when that's gone we'll have nothing at all. She's a productive asset, a profitable—"

"Stop!" His mother dabbed at her tears with her apron. "We're flat broke, Jack."

"Let's take out a loan," said Jack. "We'll pay it back by selling milk until the harvest comes in."

"A loan?" his mother said. "I promised your father I'd never take on debt!"

"Surely debt is fine if you spend it on investments or infra-structure that earns—"

"You know I run this family like a family!" his mother scolded, "and I balance the books every month. We'll sell the cow. I'm sorry to part with her, but we have no choice."

"We have a little choice," Jack muttered.

"Bring the cow to market," his mother said, firmly, "and sell her for as much as you possibly can."

So Jack took the cow and led her away, through the gate and over the hills. After a time, he passed a grand butcher's shop, with wide doors and high ceilings and even an ivy-draped turret with windows at the top, overlooking the valley.

"World's greatest steaks!" the butcher yelled from the doorway. "The best-tasting steaks in the world!" The butcher eyed Jack with interest. "Boy! Where are you leading your cow?"

"To sell in the village."

"You raised the steaks," the butcher told him, "and now it's time to raise the stakes!"

"Pardon?" Jack asked, utterly baffled. Despite his strong opinions about loans, he was a simple lad.

"Steaks as in 'meat,'" the butcher explained. "And stakes as in 'risks'."

Jack shook his head. "I still don't get it."

"Even better!" The butcher smiled, and showed Jack a handful of golden beans. "You see these? They're fantastic, believe me. Tremendous beans. They grow the best stalks, mark my words. Huge, beautiful stalks."

"That's nice," Jack said politely, though in fact he'd seen beans before.

"'Nice?'" The butcher gestured to his grand shop. "Do you want to know how I built all this?"

"Oh, yes! Please."

"It was once my father' shop. When I was a child, he gave me one cow every year until I turned eighteen. Then he gave me an entire herd. When I drove them onto a frozen pond, he gave me a whole new herd! But I'm a self-made man."

"You are?"

"The selfest," the butcher assured him. "Because while the village only grew twelvefold since my father passed, my shop is a full dozen times bigger!"

"Whoa," Jack said, with a low whistle.

"And the secret is the beans!" The butcher lowered his voice. "They're magic."

Jack begged the butcher to accept one meager cow for three priceless beans. When the butcher agreed, he nearly wept with gratitude. Pocketing the beans and patting the cow goodbye, Jack ran home to tell his mother about his good fortune.

"Well done, Jack!" his mother said, seeing that the cow was gone. "How much did you get?"

"You'll never guess."

"Ten silver pieces?" she asked.

"Better!"

A smile spread across her wrinkled face. "Fifteen?"

"Even better than that."

Her eyes glowed with happiness. "Oh, Jack. Not twenty?"

"Better than twenty," he said, showing her the magic golden beans. "I got these!"

His mother lost her patience. She grabbed the beans and tossed them out the window, where they fell in the kitchen garden. Jack tried to comfort her, but she threw her apron over her head and wept bitterly.

Then, not having anything food, they went to bed hungry.

Jack woke early the next morning with an odd sense of excitement. Noticing a shadow falling across his room, he raced to the window … but the shadow was just a dark cloud obscuring the sun.

Of course nothing had grown overnight in the garden: con-men trade in fantasies, not solutions.

With the cow gone and the harvest months away, Jack's mother was forced to sell the cottage. She moved into the poorhouse in town, where the good burghers called her a moocher and recommended that she pull herself up by her bootstraps.

Jack was luckier. He apprenticed himself to the butcher—after begging forgiveness for foolishly wasting the magic of the beans.

One day soon thereafter, as Jack packed cuts of his mother's cow into super-classy boxes, he heard the butcher sing from the high turret of his shop:

> *Fee fi fo fum,*
> *They think you're a total dum-dum.*
> *Blame those losers, be a man,*
> *Make yourself feel great again.*

Jack wanted to feel great again, he wanted his dreams to come true. He wanted to win, which meant he needed to learn more about the butcher's magic.

He ran to the ivy-covered turret and climbed and climbed till he reached the window. Peering through, he saw the butcher at an oval table, scooping gold coins into his hands then letting them pour through his short fingers.

N.T.O. Zamboni

A steady jingle came from the coins, and to Jack's shock he heard words in the clinking: every foul phrase that Jack's mother ever forbade him to say.

The coins chimed with filth about women and strangers, with the crudest terms for the sick and the foreign. And clinging to the ivy outside the window, a reckless freedom surged into Jack's heart. What if nothing was forbidden? What if nothing was his fault?

With his courage high, Jack kept watching as the butcher set the coins aside, pulled a goose from a cramped cage, and said, "Lay!"

The goose laid a golden egg.

Jack gaped. Imagine what he could do with a magic goose like that! He'd buy a new house for his mother—for every peasant—with a new cow, and chickens and pigs, too! If he waited until the butcher left the room, then stole the goose, he could—

He flushed in shame.

The butcher had treated him so kindly! First he'd given Jack magic beans, then an apprenticeship with his very own pallet in the slaughterhouse! How could he betray a man like that? And no doubt the butcher deserved every golden egg. The rich always did.

"Lay!" the butcher said again. "Lay!"

When finally the goose laid merely a silver egg, the butcher shoved it back into the cage and opened a cabinet to fetch a golden harp.

"Sing," the butcher commanded.

A heavenly voice issued from the harp: "Your dreams are dead, I'll bring them back. I alone can fix it. We need vigilance and security. I alone can fix it. The system is rigged, they're laughing at you. I alone can fix it. I alone, I alone can fix it. I am your voice, I am your voice. I alone can fix—"

Make Fairyland Great Again

"I believe!" Jack heard himself shout. "You alone can fix it!"

The butcher roared in surprise. "Fee fi fo fum!"

"Master!" Jack cried. "I believe you!"

The butcher rushed the window, swinging his cleaver. "I smell the blood of a deplorable one!"

Jack fell down and broke his crown, and the butcher carved him into chops and sold him as veal.

The Boy Who Cried Wolf

Every day a wealthy ivory-merchant sent his son to join the shepherds who tended his sheep. "Watch them carefully," his father told him.

"So they don't get lost?" the boy asked.

"Not the sheep!" the father said. "The shepherds."

"So they don't get lost?" the boy asked.

"What are you, a dummy? So they don't steal the sheep. They're nasty as hell. All of these sheep used to belong to them."

"What happened?"

"They're losers," his father explained. "And we're winners."

So the boy watched the shepherds tend the sheep in the fields near a dark forest. He called them 'grotesque' and 'disgusting,' and even punched the one playing the pipes, but they still didn't like him.

Day after day, he walked alone in the fields. He didn't get lonely, because he was too empty inside to feel loneliness, but he did get bored.

So he shouted, "Wolf! Wolf, Wolf!"

"Where?" the shepherds asked.

"Wolves!" the boy cried. "They're coming, they're coming!"

The shepherds raised the alarm, and the villagers grabbed pitchforks and rushed to protect the flock. However, when they arrived, they saw no wolves.

"Where are they?" they asked, gathering around the boy.

"In the forest," the boy told them. "There's tremendous violence in there, the animal hunger is incredible, believe me."

"You mean there are no wolves?" the town crier asked.

"I love the forest," the boy told her. "Nobody loves the forest more than me. But the wolves are pouring into the village, they're killing us. We need to take them out. We need retribution."

So the villagers patrolled the forest against these ravening beasts, and the boy's father was pleased. "With the villagers in the fields, we can save money by sending the shepherds away."

"You're fired!" the boy told the shepherds. "And you're fired, and you're fired. You're overrated, you're disgusting, you're lazy and you're a dog. Fired!"

At first, the villagers laughed at the boy's antics. However, after a few days, they stopped paying attention to every word the boy spoke.

So he grew bored again, and cried, "Wolf! Wolf!"

Once more, the villagers raced to protect the flocks, pitchforks sharp and torches bright. The shepherds joined the defense, out of a perhaps-misplaced sense of loyalty, but once more they saw no wolves. And once more, they asked, "Where are they?"

"Are you ready?" the boy asked.

The villagers didn't understand. "Ready for what?"

"We have no defenses!" the boy told them. "These wolves are beyond belief. We need to take them out. We need retribution."

N.T.O. Zamboni

"But there are no wolves," the town crier said.

"I'd like to punch you in the face. You're the most corrupt person I've ever seen. Why don't you ask what the shepherds are doing?"

"What do they have to do with anything?"

"They carry crooks! Hello? You should be ashamed of yourself. Disgusting."

"They're called crooks," a shepherd said, "but that doesn't mean—"

"Shepherds admit they carry crooks!" the town crier shouted, ringing her bell.

"I am extremely, extremely tough on wolves," the boy said. "If I were running things, there would be no wolves. None of these wolves would be rampaging in our village."

The villagers flattered and praised the boy ... but he still wanted more. He needed more. So for a third time, he cried, "Wolf! Wolf!"

And for a third time, there were no wolves.

"Where are they?" the villagers asked.

"Are you ready?" the boy asked. "To do the unthinkable to stop these cunning animals?"

"We're ready!" the villagers shouted. "Where are they?"

"Wolves in human form," the boy said, pointing to the shepherds. "And you all know what we need."

"Retribution," the villagers howled, and their pitchforks dripped with blood like fangs.

Sinbad the Sailor

Once upon a time in Baghdad, during the Addasid Caliph-
ate, a young man named Sinbad strode the streets as if he
owned them. Despite being the son of a rich and well-known
merchant, Sinbad had earned his own reputation as a young
fellow of culture, wit, and passion.

He was pretty handy with a scimitar, too.

However, Sinbad wasn't without faults. And not long after
his father's death, he squandered his inheritance on gam-
bling and poetry and romantic escapades, and found himself
penniless. So he set out to sea, in the hopes of repairing his
fortune—and perhaps of repairing himself, too.

After a few weeks, callouses formed on Sinbad's hands and
the rocking of the deck felt firmer than dry land. He swung
through the rigging and peered at the horizon, until one
morning he called, "Land ho!"

Over the next hours, an island emerged from the wispy fog;
an island that looked like a peninsula of Paradise itself. Fluted
flowers and fragrant herbs blossomed everywhere, songbirds

trilled and beehives overflowed with honey. Even better, the game animals showed no fear of the sailors.

Sinbad and his two closest friends started cooking a feast for the crew. Except as Sinbad turned the spit, a tremor dashed him to the ground.

"Back to the ship!" the master called, blowing his horn.

The earth trembled, and Sinbad ran for the shore. He stopped to help a fallen comrade when, without warning, the island plunged beneath the water—

> **DISCONTINUED IN ACCORDANCE**
>
> **WITH THE LAW FOR THE**
>
> **RESTORATION OF THE HOMELAND**

Make Fairyland Great Again

Coyote and Rattlesnake

One night while prowling the Scrub Oak Hills, Coyote chanced across a slithery snake-track in the sand. Never one to resist the bright spark of curiosity, Coyote followed the track to the home of Rattlesnake.

"Come out, come out!" he called.

"Who iss there?" Rattlesnake asked, from the darkness of her hole.

"It's me, Coyote, your neighbor."

"Coyote, you tricksster, what do you want?"

"To ask you to breakfast, of course. Come to my house tomorrow morning and I'll give you a feast!"

So the next morning, Rattlesnake slithered to Coyote's house. Coyote stood over a pot of rabbit meat, stirring and flavoring the stew. His hand shook a bit at the sight of Rattlesnake: chatting boldly to the snake at night was one thing, but seeing her movements and her rattle during the day made Coyote a little nervous.

Still, he placed a bowl of rabbit meat in front of the snake and said, "Eat, my friend."

"I do not undersstand this food of yourss," Rattlesnake told him. "I cannot eat your meat."

"What kind of food do you like?" Coyote asked.

"I like yellow cornflowers," Rattlesnake said. "And I—"

"Yellow cornflowers?" Orangutan yowled, capering toward the fire. "That's a terrible food. That's very very not tasty."

Coyote looked at Rattlesnake, and Rattlesnake looked at Coyote. They'd never seen anything so orange and brash and crude. "What are you?" Coyote asked.

"I'm the best," Orangutan sneered at Coyote. "And here's another thing you didn't know. I probably have more Indian blood than anyone around here. They don't look like Indians to me."

Rattlesnake flicked her tongue in disgust and professional jealousy. Now here was an animal who possessed true poison.

"What're you looking at, Pocahontas?" Orangutan snarled to Rattlesnake. "You know what Indians do? They bring crime and violence wherever they go! I wouldn't want them as neighbors."

Then Orangutan hurled the stew onto the ground and flung his poo at Coyote. Chortling happily, he capered away to join the animals who'd watched the whole thing.

Coyote didn't know most of them, for they'd only recently arrived in the hills.

When Orangutan beat his chest, Chicken fluttered with feverish agitation, while Cow stopped chewing her cud and rolled her eyes wildly. Ferret and Rat paced in hungry circles, Pig snorted in gleeful excitement, and earnest Donkey brayed and stomped.

Orangutan smacked his lips and groaned, roaring threats and warnings.

"Can you hear him?" Coyote asked Rattlesnake, his ears swiveling.

Make Fairyland Great Again

"My hearing iss not ssharp," Rattlesnake admitted. "He cannot be ssaying what I think."

"He is!" Coyote said. "He's warning those newcomers about ... newcomers!"

"Only I can stop the newcomers coming here and killing us!" Orangutan hooted to the newcomers. "Bringing disease and violence! Tremendous crime. Newcomers are bad, really bad. I'll remove them by force."

"Chassing away the newcomerss?" Rattlesnake asked, with a hopeful flick of her tongue. "If only he sstartss with himsself."

However, after listening to Orangutan's ranting, a solid minority of the other animals decided to put him in charge of the Scrub Oak Hills. "We're taking our country back!" They looked at Coyote and Rattlesnake. "From outsiders like them."

Goldilocks and the Three Bears

Once upon a time, three bears lived in a house in a wood: a Papa Bear, a Daddy Bear, and a Baby Bear.

Every morning, Papa Bear made three bowls of porridge and Daddy Bear drizzled honey on top of each one. And every morning, the three bears lumbered into the woods while the porridge was cooling, to collect blueberries or splash in the stream.

But one morning, after Baby Bear gamboled around a bend in the path, two young sisters with golden locks burst from the bushes.

"They're gone," said Goldilocks, the elder girl. "Let's grab their stuff!"

"I don't want their disgusting stuff," said Tuppence, the younger. "It's animals like them that make the whole forest sick."

Goldilocks didn't understand not wanting stuff, so she simply laughed and pushed through the front door. When she saw the porridge on the table, she said, "Tremendous! Some of my favorite cooks are bears."

Tuppence sneered while Goldilocks tasted a bite from the biggest bowl. "Too hot!" Goldilocks said, and tossed the porridge on the floor.

Goldilocks tasted the middle bowl. "Too cold!" she said, and threw that bowl against the wall.

Then Goldilocks tasted the third bowl. "Ooh, just right," she said, and lifted the spoon toward her mouth.

Tuppence knocked the bowl away. "Don't eat that! Bears are a grave threat to our forest."

"They are?" Goldilocks asked.

"Don't pretend you're surprised," Tuppence snapped. "You know full well what I believe."

Tuppence flounced into the living room, where she found three chairs. She didn't bother sitting in them. She knew that bears carried extremely high rates of disease brought on by the nature of their ursine practices. So she slashed the chairs with her switchblade and pulled the stuffing from cushions.

"What are you doing?" Goldilocks asked.

"Bears are degraded animals," Tuppence said. "Always whining about hunters, like they're so special."

"Well, hunters do stalk them ..."

"If they don't like being hunted, they should stop being bears!"

Goldilocks couldn't argue with that logic, so she simply followed Tuppence upstairs.

"Think they deserve special protection," Tuppence muttered, entering the bedchamber. "I'll show them what they deserve..."

A short time later, the three bears returned home—and gasped when they lumbered through the kitchen door.

"Someone's been eating my porridge," said Papa Bear, because he didn't want to mention hate crimes in front of the baby.

N.T.O. Zamboni

"Someone's been eating my porridge," said Daddy Bear.

"Someone's been eating my porridge!" giggled Baby Bear. "And they're even messier than me!"

Next, the three bears went into the living room. "Someone's been sitting in my chair!" said Papa Bear, taking Daddy Bear's hand.

"Someone's been sitting in my chair!" said Daddy Bear, struggling to keep his voice steady.

"Someone's been sitting in my chair too!" giggled Baby Bear. "And they must have a sharper butt than Mr. Porcupine!"

Finally, the three bears went upstairs into the bedroom. "Someone's been ... 'sleeping' in my bed!" said Papa Bear.

"Someone's been 'sleeping' in my bed!" said Daddy Bear, though gritted teeth.

"Someone's been sleeping in my bed too!" giggled Baby Bear. "And I think they had an accident."

"That was no accident!" Tuppence snarled from the closet. "But don't worry, being a bear is a treatable disorder."

"What—what are you doing here?" gasped Papa Bear.

"I'm going to pare away the bear." Tuppence flicked her switchblade open. "You'll be normal after I skin you alive."

The Golem of Prague

Hundreds of years ago, in the beautiful city of Prague, violence simmered outside the walls of the Jewish ghetto. The mobs called the Jews animals and savages, rapists and baby-killers. They spread lies about Jews cheering murders.

But what could the Jews do? The law didn't protect them. They were registered and identified, and kept apart from the rest of the city. The emperor smiled when the mob wielded weapons, but if a Jew even touched a knife the City Watch would slay them in the street.

Inside the ghetto walls, a holy woman named Rebbetzin Pearl mourned the violence and the fear ... yet she knew that worse was coming: a massacre, a pogrom. Something had poisoned the mood of the city. Perhaps the emperor had uttered hateful words. Perhaps the lack of jobs made the people eager to lash out at scapegoats. Either way, she needed to take action.

She locked herself in her study and prayed. She prayed through the night. When her husband knocked at the door, she scarcely heard him. She prayed through that day, and into the next night, until one word echoed in her mind: Emet.

Truth.

She flung open her study door and woke her husband and daughter. "We must create a golem," she told them. "To project the Jews against the coming violence."

Her daughter bit her lip. "But only a true tzaddik—" a holy person "—can bring a golem to life."

"What am I?" her mother responded. "Chopped liver?"

So in the moonlight, they crept through a hole in the ghetto wall.

The midnight streets of Prague were angry with curses. "Lock them up!" one man spat. "Get rid of them. Get rid of them all."

"They're not afraid of death," another man said.

"Then kill their families," a woman answered. "We're so weak. They're laughing at us. But if we kill their whole family, that'll teach them a lesson."

Rebbetzin Pearl shuddered. The yetzer hara—the urge to do evil—had been unleashed in the beautiful city.

She led her husband and daughter through a gauntlet of walls scratched with foul words and symbols. When they reached the banks of the Vltava River, they fashioned a giant figure from the heaviest clay. "Now she'll shout powerful spells from the Kabala," Pearl's husband told her daughter. "And unleash the power of life, with a blast from the heavens and the holy name of God."

However, the Rebbetzin simply beckoned quietly with her hands, inviting the Shekhina to guide her. She knelt on the bank and drew the word for 'truth' on the clay figure's forehead: Emet.

A thick fog rose from the river. The sound of the city quieted. The Rebbetzin's daughter hugged herself. And when the fog faded, she saw her mother standing beside a massive clay man who was mighty and perfect in the moonlight.

"I am here," Golem said, in a rumbling voice.

"Come," the Rebbetzin told him. "Cloak yourself in these blankets and follow us."

The Rebbetzin's daughter asked, "What is your name?"

"I have none," Golem said.

"Then I shall call you 'Emet.'"

"And I shall speak nothing else," he vowed.

When they returned to the ghetto, the Rebbetzin brought Golem to her study with her daughter. "Do you understand why I created you?" she asked Golem.

"Yes," he said.

"To protect the Jews."

"Yes," he said. "They are scared."

"The Jews?"

"The mob."

"They're scared?" the Rebbetzin's daughter asked. "They are not the ones locked in a ghetto."

"They worship authority instead of God. When you are frightened, what do you do?"

"I pray."

"So do they, and this is their prayer: 'Lock the doors, ban the strangers, and punish the deviant.'"

"You have strong opinions for a lump of clay," the Rebbetzin observed.

"I am more than a lump of clay," Golem told her. "I am a literary device in a Jewish story, and I'll tell you this: there is no golem strong enough to defeat a mob in full cry."

"What is there, then?" her daughter asked.

"Fight them before they form. There are worse things coming than pogroms, and they always start the same. With hateful words in the mouths of the powerful and hateful symbols in the streets." Golem bowed his head. "You've heard the sound of the abyss. So when the emperor says, 'I will drive them into the darkness,' believe him. He means what he says."

"Some of the things he says aren't so bad," the Rebbetzin's daughter said. "And life goes on, just the same."

"Don't be deceived by the murmuring of ordinary days," Golem said. "From a far enough distance, a massacre sounds exactly like a marketplace."

"But what if there truly is no reason to act so outraged?

"Then people will say you're silly and rude."

"I don't want them to say that!"

"We're surrounded by nice, respectful people," Rebbetzin Pearl told her, gesturing toward the city around them. "They love their families and focus on the good things in life. The scent of fresh-baked bread, the sound of a violin. They focus so well that they don't even see the ghetto walls."

"Polite people are not the blade of hatred," Golem said. "They are the scabbard."

"So what should we do?" the daughter asked.

"Survive," Golem said. "And remember—"

"The two things we do best," the Rebbetzin murmured.

"—and fight," Golem continued. "When you hear the first whisper of the abyss, fight. Never let evil grow unopposed. The first letter of the alphabet is the alef. The first letter of my name is the same. And if you lose the fight at the beginning, what is left?"

He reached to his forehead and rubbed out the alef in his name, changing emet to met—truth to death.

Rapunzel

Once upon a time, a husband and wife lived in an estate with a view of purple mountains to one side and amber fields of maize to the other. For many years they wished in vain for a child, and eventually a healthy baby girl arrived.

"We shall name her Buttercrunch!" the wife announced, holding the baby to her breast.

"After the lettuce?" her husband asked.

"How about Rapunzel?" the wife suggested.

"Much better!" her husband said.

For thirteen years, Rapunzel roamed the estate, climbing for apples in the orchard and fishing for trout in the streams. A clever, headstrong, curious girl, she read books and flew kites, and galloped her pony across the meadows. She wandered freely, beloved of the farmers and goatherds alike, and only one corner of the estate was forbidden to her.

For behind a gold-plated gate lived a powerful sorcerer from the banks of the Vulga River. And whoever stood against the sorcerer felt the crawling sensation of being smeared in a layer of slime.

Rapunzel's parents warned her against straying too close to the sorcerer's land. Now, while Rapunzel was headstrong but she wasn't stupid. She'd seen the Vulgarian in town, beating his apprentices, and felt more revulsion than curiosity.

However, the Vulgarian took an interest in her. "She's growing into a ten," he thought, peering over his fence. "What a beautiful piece of ass."

He asked her parents for permission to court Rapunzel, but they sent him away. He flaunted his wealth, to no avail. He bathed in gold coins, he whipped his apprentices, yet nothing worked. Rapunzel's parents wouldn't give her to him—and the more they refused, the more he wanted her.

So he retired to his spell-casting chamber and chanted for months over a potion of unbridled power and malice. Then he sent his apprentices into town to pour the vile brew into the well. Soon he saw the poisoned fruits of his labor. Fear spread across the land, along with suspicion, disgust, and the most powerful ingredient of all: pleasure.

For such was the genius of the Vulgarian's sorcery that he made fear and hatred feel good.

"The hordes are pushing into our city!" the Vulgarian told rapt crowds. "Sending rapists and criminals. We're weak, so weak. They're laughing at us." He brought the same message to Rapunzel's parents. "They're killing our women, viciously killing them. Our young women." He looked at Rapunzel. "Rapists and animals, savages everywhere ..."

"What shall we do?" her parents asked, sipping bespelled water from crystal goblets.

"I'll build a tower," the Vulgarian told them. "A beautiful tower. The best tower, believe me. Nobody builds greater towers. And that tower will protect everything I value."

"But ... what about us?" they asked, shaken. "The hordes are coming!"

Make Fairyland Great Again

The Vulgarian sighed. "There isn't room for everyone. However, I will save one thing of yours, whatever you love most."

What they loved most was Rapunzel, of course. So they begged the Vulgarian to protect her, and he agreed. He built his tower in a forest, with neither doors nor stairs, and only a little window high above. And with Rapunzel's parents' thanks ringing in his ears, he locked Rapunzel away.

From then on, whenever he wanted to enter, he'd stand below and call: "Rapunzel, Rapunzel, let down your hair."

And if she wanted food and drink, she'd unpin her glossy black braids and let them fall to the ground, where the Vulgarian waited to climb into her window.

After a few years and many horrors, a stalwart Dame went riding into the forest, her armor gleaming and her warhorse snorting. As she passed through a shady glen, she heard a man call:

"Rapunzel, Rapunzel, let down your hair."

She watched aghast as the Vulgarian swarmed up Rapunzel's braids to defile her. She drew her sword and waited for him to emerge. With her blade high and her eye steady, the Dame stood poised to slay the rapist, the criminal, the animal who'd spread his infectious disease.

Had two years passed since Rapunzel's abduction?

Had four?

Had eight?

Did Rapunzel still dream of freedom, of climbing for apples and fishing for trout? Or had her spirit been broken, until nothing remained of the girl she'd been?

The Dame tightened her grip on her sword and prayed that she was not too late.

The Three Little Pigs

Once upon a time, there was a fat old Sow. I'm talking a real oinker. A disgusting animal. She'd really let herself go, big league. As a young pig, she'd been a seven, and I'm being generous. Nobody's more generous than me, ask anyone.

But now? Not even a three. A two, at best.

She's some kind of single mother, I don't ask. Probably a gold-digger. Don't get me wrong, I love single mothers! Love 'em. Nobody loves single mothers more than me. They're desperate. I like that in a woman. I love women. I'm rich, so they all flirt with me, consciously or unconsciously, they can't help themselves.

This Sow has three little Pigs, and because there isn't a man around the sty, she sends them off to seek their fortune.

I give the first little pig a classy wolf whistle. The classiest. I corner her in a forest glade and make her wiggle back and forth while I give valuable suggestions. And I'm worth a lot of money, I'm huge in the forest, bigger than the trees. My suggestions are terrific.

But the first Pig is such a dummy. Instead of sticking around, she goes shaking her curly tail at a thatcher. Not a nice person. The thatcher gives her a load of straw and she builds a house. I'm a builder. I build the best houses, the best. This straw house? Crap. She doesn't have the stamina to build a good house.

I pop a Tic Tac into my mouth and knock on the door. "Little pig, little pig," I say, "let me come in."

"Not by the hair on my chinny-chin-chin," she says.

Hair on her chin? Grotesque. "Then I'll huff and I'll puff," I say, because even if she's repulsive, maybe the bitch can cook, "and I'll blow your house down."

I get into position in the outhouse and I huff and I puff. There's a whole pack of other wolves huffing and puffing with me, but they're weak and low energy. Sad!

When I huff, you can't hear anything else, that's how bigly I huff. When I puff, it's all anyone in the forest talks about for days. For weeks.

My motto is, 'any puff is good puff.' They always spell my name right, believe me.

And my favorite trick is, I wallow in the outhouse to get the best angle for huffing and puffing. Eventually the rest of the pack jumps in with me, but they're afraid of swallowing sewage.

Not me. I love the taste.

So naturally I'm the one who blows the straw house down. And I don't want to sound like a chauvinist, but when I get inside and my dinner's not on the table I absolutely go through the roof, and eat the first little pig.

Honestly, I've had better. She's a six, tops.

The next time I'm hungry, I track down the second pig. She's a little smarter than the first pig. She gathered sticks for her house, and she's inside, working on something. Stick furniture, looks like. Now, putting a woman to work is a dangerous thing. You have to treat women like shit.

So I look in the window and move on her like a bitch. "Must be a pretty picture," I say, "you dropping to your knees."

She's a nasty pig, though. So, so nasty. "Not by the hair of my chinny-chin-chin," she says.

I sniff. "Smells like you've got blood coming out of your wherever. Let me in or I'll huff and puff, and I'll blow your house down."

"Leave me alone!" she says. "Or I'll call for help!"

And she does. She squeals about my scams and my failures and all the hateful things I've done. Everyone hears, but I don't care.

Nobody cares.

I keep huffing and puffing while she rehashes boring tales about the uneducated sheep I've fleeced. The more she squeals, the more animals gather around. And the vast majority of them—almost half—want to see this uppity little porker get what's coming. The moles and bats squint eagerly, while the geese hiss and flap.

Long story short, I blow her house down and eat her face.

Pig snout? So, so good.

That's a lot of pork, so I eat other animals for a while. Not the geese, they're vicious and loyal, which is useful. But the short-sighted animals, the ones who keep chanting my name while I'm biting them in half.

There's no seasoning tastier than that.

Eventually, I get a taste for trotter. Takes me two years to find the third little pig and this one, she's a slob. A very unattractive person, inside and out. She's even got a piggy husband now, and three little pigs of her own.

She made a sturdy house of strong bricks, too, even though I'd left her nowhere to build except swampland. She spent those years organizing a team of builders and reinforcing the walls. She studied her sisters' houses, and improved the design.

But I've been busy, too. The forest is my smorgasbord. My teeth are sharp, my coat is glossy. I've even shared carcasses with my pack ... once they showed me their bellies.

I knock on the door. "Little pig, little pig, let me in."

"Not by the hair," the disgusting pig says, "of my chinny-chin-chin."

Through the window, I look right in that fat, ugly face of hers. "Then I'll huff and I'll puff and I'll blow your house in."

"Not this time," she says. "This time I'm ready."

So I huff and I puff ... but the bricks don't crack.

I wallow in sewage and huff even harder, I coat myself in filth and puff, but the house still stands.

I smile my toothiest smile. "Little pig," I say. "I know where you can find a nice field of poll-beans ripe for the plucking. If you chase after them, you'll get a tasty snack."

The pig doesn't answer, too busy talking to her piglets.

I don't mind insults. Hell, I like them. I like anger as much as I like flattery. I thrive on enemies and sycophants alike. But I can't bear being ignored. So I huff and puff, I howl and prowl ... and she keeps ignoring me.

"I will eat you!" I finally growl, and leap onto the roof.

Quick as a flash I squirm into the chimney.

I'm halfway down when I see a bubbling stew pot at the bottom, atop a roaring fire.

I dig my claws into the sides of the chimney. "You owe me an open mind!" I howl, slipping lower. "You owe me the chance to lead! I demand that you root for my success!"

"Do you?" comes the voice of the little pig.

"We're all on the same team!" I tell her, inches above the stew pot.

She peers at me through the steam. "Are we?"

N.T.O. Zamboni

"Nobody respects the rule of law more than me! Let's put aside our differences and find common ground to—"

The little pig grabs my tail and yanks me into the boiling water. "You ate my sisters, motherfucker," she says, as I shriek. "But you'll feed my kids."

www.ingramcontent.com/pod-product-compliance
Lightning Source LLC
Chambersburg PA
CBHW070642130626
46555CB00006B/2668